Anonymous

Mauch Chunk and Vicinity

with a description of the famous Switch-back railroad

Anonymous

Mauch Chunk and Vicinity
with a description of the famous Switch-back railroad

ISBN/EAN: 9783337392567

Printed in Europe, USA, Canada, Australia, Japan

Cover: Foto ©Andreas Hilbeck / pixelio.de

More available books at **www.hansebooks.com**

MAUCH CHUNK

AND

VICINITY;

WITH A DESCRIPTION OF THE FAMOUS

Switch-Back Railroad.

MAUCH CHUNK:

BOYLE, REED & GIHON.

1872.

PREFACE.

The pleasure-seeking public have long felt the need of a work descriptive of Mauch Chunk, its chief points of attraction, and the famous Switch Back Railroad. To supply this want has been the endeavor of the writer of the following pages. The wonderful attractions of this beautiful part of our State are briefly mentioned, and a history of the great and powerful Railroad and Mining Companies is given. All the facts are taken from official documents, and will be found very interesting.

(5)

Mauch Chunk and Vicinity, with a Description of The Famous Switch-Back Railroad.

MAUCH CHUNK.

Mauch Chunk, the county seat of Carbon County, Pennsylvania, is situated on the Lehigh river, forty-six miles from its mouth at Easton. It is distant eighty-nine miles from Philadelphia, from which place it is reached in about three hours, by the North Pennsylvania and Lehigh Valley, or Lehigh and Susquehanna Railroads. From New York, it is one hundred and twenty-one miles, from whence the journey occupies about four hours, by way of the Central Railroad of New Jersey and Lehigh Valley, or Lehigh and Susquehanna Railroads. Over each of these routes the journey is made without change of cars, passing through the beautiful and picturesque Lehigh Valley.

The township is composed of two boroughs, Mauch Chunk proper which lies on the western side of the Lehigh river, with Upper Mauch Chunk at the north of the old town, and at the base or on the lower portion of Mount Pisgah, and East Mauch Chunk, on an elevated plateau on the east side of the river, and opposite Mount Pisgah.

The Indian name of Mauch Chunk is " *Machk Tschunk*," or " Bear Mountain," from which it derives its name. It is a peculiar shaped mountain of considerable elevation, immediately opposite the main town, and in front of which all the passenger trains of the railroads land travellers or tourists, who design stopping here.

Mauch Chunk is the most unique town in our country, and to the lovers of the picturesque possesses many points of attraction not to be elsewhere found. It lies in a narrow gorge, surrounded by lofty mountains, and is approached from either extremity, by sharp bends in the river, and corresponding curves of the railroad tracks, so that the tourist arrives at the termination of his journey without being aware that he is near the place. This renders the first sight of Mauch Chunk's beauties, a somewhat novel one, and if the arrival is at night, the impression produced is peculiar. This feeling cannot be better described than in the words of a Western literary gentleman who lately visited here: "It was nine o'clock at night," he says, "when I was awakened from a doze by the brakesman shouting 'Mauch Chunk!' I got out hastily, and the first impression I had in my somewhat confused state was that a terrible thunder storm was coming up. I could see what I took to be dark clouds lowering all around the horizon, although the upper portion of the heavens was bright and clear. Another glance showed me, however, that the dark and portentous encirclement was mountains rising to a lofty altitude. It must be recollected that it was my first visit to the locality, and I had no conception of it. In the east, Mauch Chunk is known as the 'Switzerland of America;' I was assured of that as soon as I landed. Next day when I came to look about and see what a picturesque spot Mauch Chunk was, I blamed my own ignorance that I had never known it before, and was ready to endorse the most enthusiastic encomiums I heard pronounced upon it."

Mauch Chunk owes its origin to the enterprise of the Lehigh Coal and Navigation Company, who formerly owned the ground upon which it is situated, and who started the settlement of the place in the year 1818, from which it has grown to its present dimensions; and it now contains an industrious and thriving population of more than five thousand It is at the head of slack water navigation on the Lehigh river, along which runs the canal of the Lehigh Coal and Navigation Company, which formerly extended to White Haven, a distance of twenty-five miles further up the stream, but nearly all the dams on which were destroyed by the disastrous freshet of the fourth and fifth of June, 1862, and have not been rebuilt, the railroads being capable of doing all the carrying trade above.

THE GREAT FRESHET

Of June fourth and fifth, 1862, was one of the most noted and destructive that ever occurred in this region. The freshets on the Lehigh are of somewhat frequent occurrence after continued or heavy rains, but more generally in the spring of the year, upon the breaking up of the winter. The water caused by the melting of the snow on the mountains, flows down their sides into the river raising its volume, and at times causing much damage. Upon these occasions the current becomes very rapid and the sights presented at various points are peculiarly interesting and in some instances really grand.

In the neighborhood of Mauch Chunk, in consequence of the abrupt turns in the river, the flood frequently assumes a wild and extremely turbulent appearance, rushing, boiling and foaming with an angry noise which forcibly reminds one of the rapids above the Falls in the Niagara river. The canal and railroad tracks are frequently submerged, and the surface of the angry

1*

waters is covered by boards and heavy timbers, from the destruction of rafts, cabins, &c., above, which are brought down the fierce stream with a velocity that is almost terrific.

The '62 freshet was one which will long be remembered by those who lived in Mauch Chunk and its neighborhood at that time. A severe storm of rain was raging, when on the fourth of June it was observed that the river was beginning to rise and its body to rapidly swell. This continued during the day and all through the long night Higher and higher—broader and broader—wider and wider—fiercer and fiercer became the angry flood—and when daylight broke on the morning of the fifth, the people began to feel the apprehension of real danger. As the day advanced the water continued to rise, the canal banks and railroad tracks had entirely disappeared, huge timbers, parts of houses, bridges and broken canal boats, rushed with headlong fury down the stream—now floating on its surface, then sinking beneath, now raised to upright positions and anon dashed down with great fury—to pursue their way down the swollen and turbulent stream, producing still further destruction. The boom in the river at White Haven had early given way—dam after dam had followed it,—the road bridge in front of the Mansion House, and the iron bridge one mile below, where the Lehigh Valley Railroad crosses, were all carried away by the force of this fell besom of destruction. Persons living and working along the shores of the river, and the hands belonging to the canal boats were in many cases swept away, not having time to leave their houses or boats to flee to the hills for safety; while others barely saved their lives, leaving their property to be destroyed by the pitiless waters. In Mauch Chunk, Susquehanna street had become part of the river, and the tide had rapidly inundated all the cellars and fast filled up the lower stories of the houses. At the Mansion House the scene was one of intense excitement. The first story was entirely filled, and the water was beginning to show itself on the second floor, and continued to rise there until it had attained a depth of twenty-eight inches in the dining-room. Here dismay seized upon the boarders and others in the house, and many of them repaired to the bowling saloon, on the mountain in the rear of the house, for safety. A canal boat in its rapid career down the stream struck a corner of the Mansion House, bounded away again, and pursued its headlong reckless course onward.

Many lives were lost during this appalling time, and many hair breadth escapes from death occurred. One of these latter we will mention. Mr. Yeager, who kept a store on Susquehanna street, in endeavoring to escape from it to get to his home on Broadway, thinking he could stem the fierce current which was rushing down the street, stepped into the raging flood, was at once carried off his feet and hurried along by its resistless force beyond the Mansion House, and past the railroad bridge below; here he succeeded in catching hold of and getting on a canal boat, which carried him past Parryville, six miles below. Luckily the boat struck the side of a mountain, when he succeeded in grasping hold of the branches of a tree, from which he climbed to a place of safety, and was fortunate enough to make his way to Parryville.

"THE SWITZERLAND OF AMERICA."

The picturesque scenery in the neighborhood of
Mauch Chunk—its wild, varied and romantic
beauty—has given it, and not inaptly, as has been
already stated, the generally received appellation
of "The Switzerland of America." The traveller's first view of it is like the lifting of a curtain
before a strange and beautiful picture, he is at
once in the middle of the quaint environs of a
magic circle, he must be right in the town before
he can see it—walled in as it is by the masonry
of nature, with huge rocks scattered here and
there and projecting at various points, of the surrounding mountains, whose sides and summits are
covered with the towering forms of beautiful
trees clad in eternal foliage. How pitiful and in-
significant are the greatest of the works of men,
when compared with scenes as glorious as these!
Oh! these real grand sights of nature's handiwork,
how they charm the inmost soul; and thought,
lost in admiration ascends in adoration from
such sublime works to a contemplation of the

mightiness of their Architect! But it is not only in the summer season when these glorious hills are clothed in living green, that the tourist can see and enjoy the great beauties of this interesting portion of our country. Every season develops its peculiar beauties, and each has its own attractions. The accomplished editor of the "Philadelphia Sunday Mercury," in speaking of a visit to this place, says: "By every European traveller is recognized the superior beauty—to that of every other part of the temperate zone— of the autumn scenery of the Middle States. The October landscapes of the corresponding latitude in England are sombre. They tell of sadness, decadence, death and decay. The picture of an American autumn, is a picture dressed in all the hues of the most gorgeous sunset. The European landscape in October, might well be used to typify the death of a man having no hope of a beatific future. For the departure from this world of one who had lived a life of usefulness to his fellow-men, and of service to his Creator, we could select no more fitting symbol than the expiring splendor of the foliage of an American forest. Recognizing this beauty in our scenery, the Dusseldorf Academy is now immortalizing on canvas the enrapturing views in the vicinity of Mauch Chunk. To sketch the principal scenes in this locality, and of the valley in general, by this appreciative and discerning school of art, the celebrated Hertzog has been dispatched. To a recognition of the natural beauties of Mauch Chunk, it is quite time that the attention of our own people was more generally directed. Upon the American Guide Books published in London, Paris and Berlin, it is described, and truly so, as of all American towns very far the most picturesque. The region in which it lies is the 'Switzerland of America.' Between the lofty hills, in a narrow gorge, the town is nestled ; so compact, that upon one narrow street its entire houses impinge. Of gardens, the residents, excepting what ground they can rescue from the hills above their heads, have not one foot of space.

" A visit to it will repay an hundred-fold both its time and its cost. What is remarkable is, that by European tourists, the beauties of Mauch Chunk are better known, than by Americans who can talk with glibness of St. Bernard, of the Myringen, or of Berne."

This latter point exhibits one of the peculiar characteristics of the American people. While they are frequently very imperfectly acquainted with the extent, grandeur and beauty of their own country, which is unparalleled for its many and varied objects of natural splendor, and innumerable curiosities (with its lofty mountains, its beautiful and fertile valleys, its broad prairies, its majestic and almost endless forests, its lofty waterfalls, its mighty lakes and noble rivers), many of which are immediately around them, they can talk volubly of their travels in London, Paris and Switzerland, of the grandeur of the Alps, of the balmy atmosphere and gorgeous skies of Italy, of the wonders of Vesuvius, and other places of like European celebrity—and yet they have never seen, and know nothing of the beauties of far greater interest within a few hours' ride of their own homes. Why do our people waste their time and money in making the tour of Europe, enduring hardships, dangers and many mortifications, when they have greater sources of interest and curiosity, and more enticing scenes so near them and of such easy access ?'

To the lover of science, and the student who wishes to study the mysteries which are buried in the bowels of the earth; to the lover of the beauties of nature; to the overworked citizens of our populous cities, who require relaxation from mental or physical labor and a place of delightful rest; to pleasure-seekers; and to those who desire to preserve their health, or to repair that which is impaired, we know of no place more deserving of attention than Mauch Chunk and its vicinity. Here can be found delightful drives, numerous roads for pleasant and invigorating walks, good fare, pure water, and the bracing mountain air, all promotive of cheerfulness and sound health.

THE COAL TRAFFIC.

If you are not too fond of exertion, you may sit cozily in your "Easy Chair" on the veranda of the Mansion House, enjoying the beautiful scenery around you, and get some slight idea of the wonderful activity and extent of the great Lehigh coal trade, a sight in itself fully worth the time, labor and cost of a visit to this delightful and almost magic region. Immediately in front of you flows the beautiful and sometimes turbulent Lehigh, with its numerous tracks of railway on both shores, and the canal on the opposite side, all busy with their continuous and numerous cars and boats filled with the coal which has just been taken from the mines in the immediate neighborhood. A writer in one of the New York illustrated journals, describing the view from this position, says, you can see "just where the turbulent Lehigh sweeps around, as if to give the town a salute, and then rushes off merrily again. One sees the river, a canal, two railways, a road and a street packed in a space scarcely more than a stone's throw wide. The hurrying river, busy canal, railways and highway lie crowded between the steep hills. Here there is always the stir of a great traffic. Ceaselessly, day and night, long coal trains come winding around the base of the hills like so many huge anacondas, often with head and tail lost to the eye, the locomotive reaching out of sight before the last car comes swinging around the curve. These trains are of marvellous length, sometimes numbering over two hundred cars. So continuous is their coming and going, that usually several trains are visible at the same time, and rarely at any moment is the whistle or the puff of the locomotive silent." These trains are almost exclusively employed in freighting coal; and this immense traffic in black diamonds becomes still more surprising when it is remembered that in addition to the trains, canal boats similarly freighted ceaselessly pass with the regularity, order and succession of a procession. We may watch the stirring traffic, the quiet canal, the swift Lehigh,—sometimes only the small thread of a river barely covering its rocky bed, but occasionally a roaring flood bringing ruin upon its surface and carrying ruin before it—or we may study the tints and forms of the receding mountains.

The great business of the place is coal. The Lehigh coal. Men, women and children talk coal, buy coal, sell coal or handle coal. It is dug out, sorted over, screened, worked, weighed, dumped into cars and boats day after day, month after month, till the only steady music is the splash of water over the dam, the rumble of cars and the rattle of coal.

An idea of the business may be had when it is known that the coal business of this place gives life and profit to the Lehigh Coal and Navigation Company, with its twenty million dollars capital, and to the Lehigh Valley Railroad, with its eighteen million dollars capital; all well and profitably invested.

In the year 1870, both roads and canal shipped the enormous quantity of five million seven hundred and sixty-five thousand five hundred and sixty-four (5,765.564) tons, being an average of a little more than nineteen thousand two hundred and eighteen (19,218) tons per day, allowing three hundred working days to the year. Owing to the strike of six months' duration in 1871, we give the official figures of 1870.

It is well known to the reader that of late years there have been several strikes by the miners and laborers in the coal regions throughout the country, which have led to a suspension of all operations at the mines, and also that this section of the country has been the scene of some of these unfortunate difficulties. On the tenth of January, 1871, the second general suspension of mining took place here, and lasted until about the first of July, causing great loss not only to the operators and miners, but to the great number of iron manufacturers in the Lehigh Valley and elsewhere, and in fact to all engaged in business of every kind in the coal regions

MANUFACTORIES, BANKS, &C.

But independent of the coal traffic there is considerable other business done in Mauch Chunk, in which a large amount of capital and a great number of persons are employed. The Mauch Chunk Iron Works at the head of the town, owned and operated by Albright and Stroh, is a very extensive establishment. During the late war it did a large business in the manufacture of heavy shot, shell, &c. J. H. Salkeld and Co., are also heavily engaged in the iron business, and their machine shops and foundry turn out an immense quantity of heavy castings and costly machinery. At the Hazard Manufacturing Co., every variety of iron wire and iron rope is made, and large orders are constantly being received and filled from all sections of the country. Of financial institutions there are, the First National Bank, Second National Bank, the Banking House of G. B. Linderman and Co., and some smaller institutions. Charters have also been granted by the Legislature for other banks to be located here.

There are a number of hotels here, among which may be noticed the Mansion House and the American Hotel, both excellent establishments, where travellers can be comfortably and even sumptuously entertained.

Three first-class weekly newspapers are published here, the Mauch Chunk Coal Gazette, by Boyle, Reed and Gihon, the Mauch Chunk Democrat, by Jos. Lynn, and the Carbon Democrat, by an Association. The first devotes much of its attention to coal and iron matters, and in politics is Republican, the two latter are Democratic.

CHURCHES

There are several fine churches here. St. Mark's Protestant Episcopal Church, is one of the handsomest structures for religious worship in the State. It is built of stone, and stands upon a solid foundation on a terrace on the side of the mountain, in Race street. It is surmounted by a beautiful tower and spire, which rises to a height of one hundred and thirty-five feet. It has a superior organ, and its interior is a model of elegance in all its appointments. It cost over seventy thousand dollars; but through the liberality of those who contributed to its erection, its seats are at all times *free* to all who desire to worship there. The rector is the Rev. Leighton Coleman, who will at any time furnish facilities for strangers to view the interior of this beautiful building. There are also a large and handsome Presbyterian, a Methodist Episcopal, a German Reformed and a Roman Catholic Church, all of which are well attended and liberally supported.

Of benevolent and other societies this town can boast of more than any other of its size in the State.

PRIVATE RESIDENCES.

We have spoken of the cramped appearance of the town, its houses being mostly built against the side of the mountains, with but little room for gardens or other outside ornamentation. All this is true, yet there are in Mauch Chunk many buildings not only comfortable and commodious, but some of them really elegant, and showing evidences of fine taste. A walk along Broadway presents many such attractive places to the visitor's view. And if he will walk up to the head of Susquehanna street, passing the Post Office, Court House and County offices, he will find directly before him on the rising hill side, the splendid residence of the Hon. John Leisenring. This fine mansion is surrounded by beautifully and artistically laid out grounds, commanding a view of the town and river. Judge Leisenring is largely interested in coal and railroad enterprises in this vicinity, and has done much towards its present healthy condition and its permanent prosperity. Above and adjoining this on the left, we have the substantial and elegant mansion of the Hon. Asa Packer. This gentleman is known throughout the Union as one of the most successful coal and railroad operators in the country. For the entire Lehigh Valley, and Mauch Chunk especially, he has done much, and is deservedly esteemed for it. He has consequently, on numerous occasions been placed in offices of honor and trust by his fellow-citizens, and at all times has filled such positions with credit to himself and to their entire satisfaction. Judge Packer was a representative in Congress from 1853 to 1857, and although not a talker, was what is far better, a worker, and one of the most useful members of the House. He is shrew, industrious and indefatigable in everything he undertakes; his untiring energy and great business abilities have led to the possession of immense wealth. This wealth he knows how to use properly, and like those other great American philanthropists, George Peabody and Peter Cooper,

2

he is determined to see some of the great good
that can be done with a portion of it during his
own lifetime. Judge Packer, in 1865, donated a
fine tract of fifty-six acres of valuable land in
South Bethlehem, on which to erect buildings
for the education of young men in the higher
branches of collegiate knowledge, and especially
in such branches as Engineering, Civil, Mechanical and Mining; Chemistry, Metallurgy, Archi-
tecture and Construction

Beside the ground, he gave five hundred thousand dollars for the purpose of erecting the requi-
site buildings and placing its environs in proper
order, and the purchase of apparatus, &c. This
institution which is known as the "Lehigh Uni-
versity," was formally opened on September first,
1866. The President of the Board of Trustees is
the Right Rev. Wm. Bacon Stevens, D. D., LLD.,
Bishop of Pennsylvania, and the President of
the Faculty is Henry Coppee, LL.D. The institution is now in successful working order, having
in addition to its learned President, a faculty of
the highest order of intellect. Judge Packer, not
satisfied, however, with his first munificent gifts,

MANSION HOUSE, MAUCH CHUNK.

E. T. Booth, Proprietor.

has further endowed it with a fund sufficient to
make it a free institution, where all the instruc-
tion imparted is given without cost to the
student.

THE MANSION HOUSE,

Situated on the banks of the Lehigh river, is
a handsome and imposing structure immediately
in front of the west bank of the Lehigh river,
having only a street and the track of the Lehigh
and Susquehanna Railroad separating it from
that stream. Directly opposite, on the east side
of the river (over which there is here a good free
bridge), rises Bear Mountain, with its tall dark
round top, and at the foot of which are the tracks
of the Lehigh Valley Railroad, where also is
situated the new and handsome depot of that
road. All the passenger trains of both roads stop
in front of the Mansion House.

It has a frontage of two hundred and seventy-
five feet and is five stories high. On the second
story front it has a wide and comfortable piazza

running the whole length of the building, where visitors can sit and breathe the fresh air, enjoying a sight of the river with its magnificent surrounding scenery.

The Mansion House is in every respect a first-class hotel. It has several large sitting and reading rooms for gentlemen, and its splendid parlors are furnished in the most costly and elegant manner, and in the best possible taste. The dining-room on the same floor, is large, light and cheerful, and is a model of cleanliness and good order. The tables are literally furnished with all the delicacies of the season, served in a manner not to be surpassed. The rooms, one hundred and sixty-six in number, are all well lighted and ventilated, and furnished in the best and most comfortable style.

Of the proprietor of this model establishment, Mr. E. T. Booth, we hardly know what to say. His good natured smiling face is apparently to be seen in all parts of the house at the same time, and he is always attentive to the wants, and looks after the pleasure of his guests. He certainly " knows how to keep a hotel," and uses all his endeavors to make this one so attractive, that all who visit it once will desire to do so again. At the south end of the house is a never failing mineral spring of pure cool water, as clear as crystal. Its medicinal qualities have been highly commended.

The "Switch Back" will be kept in operation with many new attractions, and the opportunity of enjoying this romantic ride will be improved by thousands, especially if they can unite with this pleasure the essentials of a good hotel, fine rooms, and a well prepared table, all of which they have in the Mansion House.

PROSPECT ROCK.

No one should leave Mauch Chunk without visiting Prospect Rock, one of its chief attractions.

It is a ledge of rocks projecting from the side of the mountain south of the Mansion House, and is reached by a few minutes' walk from the piazza of the hotel.

Here the lover of the beautiful in nature can

spend hours reclining on the rocks beneath the
cool shade of the trees, with a magnificent and
ever changing panorama of romantic scenery
unfolded in every direction at his feet. Down
the river through the narrows, directly opposite
" Bear Mountain," with the Lehigh Valley Railroad winding its way around the sharp curve, and
the depot nestled at its base; between the river
and railroad the canal with its boats loaded and
unloaded, passing and repassing. To the right
looking up the river may be seen the coal pockets,
East Mauch Chunk, and Broad Mountain in the
distance. To the left lies the town under the
cool shadows of the mountain, St. Mark's Episcopal Church and the beautiful residences of Hon.
Asa Packer and Judge Leisenring, prominently
visible on the hill side. Whilst beneath, all is
alive with the hum and bustle of life, above, on
the brow of the hill in the sunlight are seen the
marble columns marking the "city of the dead."

THE FLAG STAFF.

Above "Prospect Rock" upon the summit of
the mountain is an immense ledge of rocks, better
known as the Flag Staff, and, next to "Mount
Pisgah," is the highest point in the Lehigh
Valley.

It is well worth a visit, and is reached by
"Donkey Path" in the rear of the Mansion
House after a brisk walk of half an hour. Its
name is derived from the following incident:
Upon the very summit stood a hemlock tree in
all its stately grandeur, until one day during a
severe storm it was struck by lightning which
divested it of its limbs, leaving the trunk unin-
jured. At the opening of the late civil war a
party of patriotic young men nailed to this staff
a flag, bearing the stars and stripes, which here
remained unfurled to the breeze until it was torn
to shreds by the bleak winter storms. During
the late Franco-Prussian war some sympa-
thizing friends unfurled the Prussian flag from
this same staff, but this was destined to a sad

2*

fate, as on the following night the sympathizers with the French cut down this famous Flag Staff.

To adequately depict from this point the view, extending to the horizon beyond, very considerably transcends the power of pen. They to whom is familiar Edward Everett's pen picture of the view from Mount Washington, may elicit from it some glimmering idea of the panorama beheld from the Flag Staff. The stirring coal traffic, the great canal, the rapid Lehigh, the fumes from the locomotive funnel, and the tints and forms of the receding hills, go to make up a picture of such sublimity that no tourist should leave Mauch Chunk until he has feasted upon its beauties.

By next year this spot will be reached by a wagon road from the Mansion House.

MOORE'S RAVINE.

To the lovers of wild and rugged scenery a journey to Moore's Ravine will amply repay the trouble of a visit.

This beautiful and enchanting place is situated about two miles above Mauch Chunk. It consists of a succession of waterfalls and cascades, the highest fall being seventy-five feet. Every portion of the ravine is of the wildest and most romantic character. The gorge varies in different places from a few feet to seventy or eighty feet in width, and extends from the bottom to the summit of Broad Mountain, a height of about one thousand feet. Those who wish to do so can ascend, by at times following a foot path, and at different points crossing the gorge on pieces of broken rocks or fallen trees. In this way all the startling and transcendant beauties of the several falls can be seen to advantage—the water now flowing in a gentle ripple, then a quiet beautiful rivulet, and anon a fierce torrent rushing through a narrow pass and falling on the rocks below, dashing its sparkling spray on everything around, and shining like so many brilliant gems in the bright sunlight. From every point the view is charming and in many places it is truly grand.

Owing to the wildness of this place it is only accessible to the tourist who is " seeking pleasure under great difficulties." It is, however, contemplated to have this gorge opened and made accessible to all.

LENTZ'S TROUT PONDS.

These celebrated trout ponds are the property of Mr. La Fayette Lentz, of Mauch Chunk, one of the most successful brook trout culturists in the State, and are located in Beaver Run Valley, a short distance from Packerton, a pleasant drive of several miles from Mauch Chunk along the mountain road and up the valley, passing on the way Judge Packer's deer park.

The ponds are in the charge of Mr. Alfred Lentz (a brother to the proprietor), and are constructed at intervals of from fifty to two hundred yards; in which are placed the trout of different growths. Near the residence of Mr. Lentz, a few feet from the road, stands the hatching-house, which is built over the stream, and contains six sets of covered wooden boxes; over the bottom, which is composed of white gravel, flows the pure sparkling water from a spring situated at the head of the hatching-house.

On the arrival of the spawning season the eggs are artificially removed from the female trout of mature growth, and placed in the hatching-boxes, which are divided into different apartments along the length of the room. The first apartments contain the trout in embryo, the next those a little farther advanced, and so on, comprising thousands of baby trout (looking like specks of coal dirt), which keep themselves huddled together in groups in the corners of the boxes. As they grow older they are removed from one apartment to another until they eventually reach the water of the pond below. An even temperature is kept up in the room during the spawning season through the fall and winter. There are about two hundred and fifty thousand trout in the hatching boxes, in different stages of maturity.

The creek which flows through the farm contains about two hundred and fifty thousand more, so that it can be safely said that the total number of trout in the stream, ponds and hatching-house is five hundred thousand. There are eight ponds along this stream, each of which is alive with these speckled beauties. In the lower ponds, which contain the larger trout, may be seen some measuring two feet and weighing five pounds. The trout are fed about six times a day; this frequent feeding is to prevent the larger ones from eating up the smaller, and is a sight well worth seeing, as the moment the food touches the water hundreds of them instantly rise to the surface and take it with their well known greediness. Some of the larger trout have become so accustomed to being fed that they will eat out of the hand.

Mr. Lentz is always ready to receive visitors in his kind and courteous style, conduct them through his grounds, and explain all matters of interest to them.

A TRIP AROUND THE SWITCH BACK RAILROAD.

One of the greatest attractions that can be offered to the tourist is a ride on the famous "Gravity Railroad."

Before making this interesting journey, however, it will not be out of place to give a short historical sketch of the

DISCOVERY OF COAL

in this region, as it was this great discovery that led to the necessity for the construction of this important and very ingenious piece of engineering skill.

In the latter part of the last century the whole of this portion of the country was little more than an unexplored wilderness, and scarcely inhabited by a civilized being, excepting here and there an isolated squatter, who lived a kind of aboriginal life, eking out a scanty livelihood by hunting. The bear, the deer, and other wild animals were the principal living things to be found in the neighborhood. At this period a hardy and adventurous pioneer named Philip Ginter settled in this district, built himself a rude hut, and supported his family by the use of his gun. One day in one of his numerous rambles over the hills in search of game, without succeeding in finding any, he was returning home towards night in a somewhat despondent mood, when he found at the roots of a tree which had recently been blown down, some pieces of a black hard substance which attracted his attention, and having heard it frequently surmised that coal existed in the neighborhood, it occurred to him that this might be some of that veritable substance. This was in the vicinity of what is now known as "Summit Hill," and the period, the year 1791. He gathered some specimens of these black stones, and submitted them to the examination of Col. Jacob Weiss, residing at what was then known by the name of Fort Allen, now Weissport

Unable to determine its real character, the Colonel took the specimens with him to Philadelphia, where after undergoing the scrutiny of sundry mineralogists and learned savans it finally came into the hands of Charles Cist, a printer, who pronounced it stone coal, and authorized the Colonel to satisfy Ginter for his discovery upon his pointing out the precise spot where he found the coal.

It was first called black stone, and for a long time its combustible qualities were denied. Experiments were made with it in Philadelphia and elsewhere, and it was asserted that this hard rocky substance, which resembled coal, only served to put the fire out. Soft coal could easily be ignited and rapidly consumed, but it was declared that this hard anthracite coal could not be made to burn. Further experiments were however made, until at last it was found that this black stone although more difficult to ignite than the soft bituminous coal, possessed decided combustible qualities, and that the discovery was a valuable one. A company was soon formed and opened a mine on Sharp Mountain. In consequence of not knowing how to use it, the prejudice against this coal was so great that but little progress was made in mining and obtaining a market for it until the year 1820, when the shipments of it from this region began to be a matter of some importance. But the difficulties and expense of transportation even then were matters which acted as great preventatives to the proper working of the mines, or in a manner to yield any considerable profit. The coal was taken slowly and tediously from the mines, a distance of nine miles to the river, in wagons, the work of transportation being found to be more laborious and expensive than that of mining. This mode of conveying the coal from the mines continued until 1827, when the

SWITCH BACK RAILROAD

was constructed with a descending grade from Summit Hill to the Lehigh river, on which the cars were run down by their own gravity, being brought back by mules, which were brought down the mountain with each descending train of cars in a sort of crate or cattle car. This road was called the gravity road, and is believed to be the first road ever laid out with an instrument.

The demand for coal from these mines increased to such an extent that it was found necessary to adopt a more expeditious mode of transportation, and in 1844 the mule system was given up, and the plan of a back track or "Switch Back," with planes, was adopted, and is in use at the present time.

THE TRIP

Coaches leave the Mansion House to convey passengers to the foot of "Mt. Pisgah Plane." The ride to this place is a very pleasant one, the coach rattles through the street, diverges into the road that ascends the hill, giving a very fair view of the town, and after a journey that the impatient traveller imagines must have already taken him to the top of the mountain, draws up at the foot of the plane. But to those who wish to embrace the opportunity of getting a better view of surrounding objects, and of observing some of the operations of the Lehigh Coal and Navigation Company, we would say make the journey on foot, the distance not being great and the walk an agreeable and instructive one. Leaving the Mansion House we walk up Susquehanna street along the Lehigh river, till we pass the Court House, where a road leads up the side of the mountain to Upper Mauch Chunk. On our way we pass the handsome residences and grounds of Hon. Asa Packer on our left, and Hon. John

Leisenring on our right. Further up the hill we have a good view of the inclined planes and the shutes by which the coal is lowered from the top of the mountain to the river below, and there separated into the different sizes of nut, stove, egg, broken, &c., and finally deposited in cars or boats ready for shipment to market. The coal shutes, or dumps, are of themselves objects of no little interest. All these thousands, aye millions of tons of coal come down this mountain in cars holding about three tons each, let down on one track by a wire rope, the loaded car descending drawing an empty car from the shutes on the river bank to the summit of the hill, whence they are brought direct from the mines, then lowered in turn to draw up those which just went down ladened. This going up and coming down is continued all the day long with the regularity of clock work, so perfect is the arrangement for shipping coal, and so mechanical and perfect in their work have become the men employed by the Company. After viewing the things just described, we continue our walk around the brow of the hill, until we arrive at the foot of

VIEW OF MAUCH CHUNK AND MOUNT PISGAH.

MT. PISGAH PLANE.

In looking up at this formidable place of ascent for the first time, the visitor feels somewhat timid about going up, but there is no cause whatever for the slightest apprehension of danger. The plane is twenty-three hundred and twenty-two (2322) feet in length, with an elevation of six hundred and sixty-four (664) feet, being a rise of about one foot in three. There are two tracks and upon each runs a " safety-car," to which is attached heavy steel bands, each seven and one-half inches wide. These bands are fastened to iron drums twenty-eight feet in diameter in the engine-house at the head of the plane, the motive power being two stationary engines of one hundred and twenty horse-power each. The safety-car has attached to it an iron arm, which extends from the side of the car over a ratchet-rail between the two tracks. Should the band break or any accident happen to the machinery, the least backward movement causes the arm to drop into the notches of the safety-rail, holding the train stationary. In all the years that this enterprise has been in opera tion, not a single passenger has met with accident going up this mountain. This speaks well for the management, as well as for the ingenuity of the invention, which may well claim to be perfection itself.

We now take our seats in one of the comfortable little passenger cars, the conductor stations himself upon the platform of the front car, the signal is given to the engineer at the head of the plane, the safety-car is drawn slowly from the pit behind the cars and the train begins to ascend until we arrive at the top, where the party alights to take a look around at the enchanting sight which here presents itself. Mr. Henry in his " History of the Lehigh Valley" says of this ride: " Up, up we go until the mountain tops which just now towered above us, sink into the valleys and become pigmy hills, and the whole face of the surrounding country in an immense circuit opens under us like one vast flower-bed, enriched with all the glowing garb of autumn, and glittering in the sunlight which intensifies every beauty

and color. Novel emotions crowd upon the mind
as the enchanting and exciting scene unfolds itself
with new and almost appalling grandeur as the
summit is approached, and the soul is transported
with awe as the works of the Creator stand out
in their imposing contrast to our littleness as we
hang suspended as it were in mid-air. We have
now reached the summit of Mt. Pisgah, and attained an elevation of thirteen hundred and
seventy (1370) feet above tide water. And now
what a glorious, what a sublime, what a varied
landscape bursts upon the enraptured vision!
The Blue Mountains, the Lehigh Water Gap,
through which may be seen far distant hills, in-
cluding on a clear day Schooley's Mountain in
New Jersey, a distance of fifty-six miles. In all
other directions mountains in long ranges piled on
other mountains; beneath, the towns, which look
like groups of toy-houses, but from which and
the river ascends the busy sounds of industry, the
voices of men, the whistling of steam-engines, the
boatman's merry horn, the rattling of coal as it
goes down the shutes into the boats, while in a
bass accompaniment to this industrial music

3

there is a continuous rumbling of cars up and down the planes and along the level railroads."

Another most excellent writer, in speaking of the view from the top of Mt. Pisgah, says: " Yes, that is Mauch Chunk. Down in that twisting, serpentine ravine just under us. Down, down in the gorge between the mountain sides, the sun on a hot day reflecting first from one side, then from the other, till it seems as if the village would be parboiled every twenty-four hours, and then washed down into the Lehigh, should there come a drenching rain storm to start the currents of rushing water down the sides of the mountains, rising high and abruptly on either side.

Mountains and valleys, hills and ravines, little villages and mining settlements below us, with long blue ridges of mountains rising all about us as far as the eye can reach attract the tourist and add to the novelty of the scene.

Everything seems to have been twisted and scrunched and hurled and piled together, then turned, piled and hurled together again, as if the elements of nature had been in rebellion when this part of the country was finished or perfected, if we may call this rugged, broken grandeur below us and far outreaching, the perfection of nature !"

It is in contemplation to erect on the summit of Mt. Pisgah, a handsome pavillion for the accommodation of persons riding over the " Switch-Back," so as to enable any who desire, to refresh themselves, and enjoy quietly and pleasantly the magnificent prospect spread out beneath them.

Again taking our seats in the cars the train starts on the gravity road, on a down grade of fifty feet to the mile. After a swift and exhilarating ride of six miles the foot of Mt. Jefferson is reached, having descended in that distance three hundred feet.

MT. JEFFERSON.

The ascending plane here is two thousand and seventy (2070) feet long, overcoming a height of four hundred and sixty-two (462) feet. The train is again attached to a safety-car and drawn to the top of the mountain, which is the highest point on the road, being sixteen hundred and thirty-five (1635) feet above tide-water. After a short ride we arrive at

SUMMIT HILL,

the principal mining town in the Lehigh coal region. It contains about two thousand inhabitants, composed principally of miners and their families, and those who supply them with the necessaries of life. It has a dismal looking town-hall, in appearance resembling a French Bastile, which is one of the first things which attracts the visitor's attention. The town has a neat and comfortable appearance, and has a fair supply of churches, schools and hotels. Many persons who desire a pleasant retreat, with pure, wholesome mountain air, make this a place of summer sojourn. As we already remarked, it was near this town that coal was first discovered by Ginter in 1791, and it was here also that the first mine was worked by the Lehigh Coal and Navigation Company. From this place we have a view of the Panther Creek Valley, which is the very heart of the anthracite coal region

In this valley can still be seen the grading, etc., of what was part of the old " Switch-Back," used for making the descent into the valley by gravity, the cars being again drawn up to Summit Hill by another plane.

Here are located the mines and breakers (ten in number) of the Lehigh Coal and Navigation Company. Those who wish to do so have the opportunity of visiting any of the mines, which they can enter with experienced guides, and view the mysteries and dangers of life underground. The coal-breakers when in operation are objects of no little curiosity. These are huge pieces of machinery where the coal is broken up from large lumps into smaller and more marketable sizes. Here may be seen scores of merry, bright-eyed, dirty little urchins, who are employed to pick out from the coal all stone, slate and other impurities, which have passed through the breakers. In this occupation they become very expert, and though to an inexperienced observer they appear to be paying but little attention to the business before them, their work is generally done with considerable care and accuracy.

The immense mounds of coal dust around the mines fill all who see them with surprise and regret at the apparent waste, but the Anthracite Fuel Manufacturing Company are now in successful operation, working up this formerly useless coal dust into fuel for market. These mounds give a dreary look to the valley, killing all vegetation, and causing the creeks to run streams as black as ink.

UTILIZATION OF COAL DUST.

In addition to the Company already mentioned as being in operation for the utilization of coal dust, a number of interesting experiments having this end in view, have been made by other parties. The committee on " Arts and Sciences" of the Franklin Institute of the State of Pennsylvania having examined a number of specimens of artificial fuel prepared by Mr. E. F. Loiseau, of Philadelphia, report that they have made trials of the samples procured, and that they are well adapted for purposes in which intensity of combustion is not desired. For the production of steam in stationary boilers and for household purposes, it can be used equally as well as any ordinary coal;

and whenever the cost of preparation is less than the cost of mining coal, this invention will make available the immense amounts of small coal allowed to remain useless at the coal mines and will probably come into use.

THE BURNING MINE.

We will now visit the burning mine close by, which has been on fire since the year 1832, and thousands of dollars have been expended in endeavoring to extinguish it. The effects of the fire and its accompanying heat are almost as well shown here as at Vesuvius and Etna. The rocks are baked, and of every shade of color, they have changed their stratified position and are reclining in every conceivable way.

THE RETURN.

We take the old mule track route back to Mauch Chunk, a distance of nine miles, with an average grade of ninety-six feet to the mile, and in about thirty minutes we find ourselves again in Upper Mauch Chunk, at the foot of Mt. Pisgah, the place from which we started.

"Brick Pomeroy," who recently made this journey, says (and we think that all others who have done so will heartily coincide with him): "This ride was most delightful. No noise, no rumbling, liability of explosion or colliding with a train or car going in an opposite direction. It is all one way here. The cars are pulled up, and down they go of their own accord. The route is up hill and down, over a rugged uncultivated country. Rocks, stones, mountains, ravines, hills, cliffs; rocks, stones, declivities; hills, rocks, mountains, broken rocks, gorges; big rocks, ravines, little rocks, mountains; rocks set up end-wise and stuck in edge-wise, and you have a very good picture of the crooked, circuitous route by which we went and came on this the pleasantest railroad ride in our life."

An interesting time to take a trip around the Switch-Back is on a moonlight night. This is occasionally done when parties of excursionists desire it, and is highly enjoyed.

As novel and entertaining as this excursion is

duiing the summer season, its interest, beauty and
pleasure are enhanced by a visit to and over the
road in the autumn. Riding around the mountain with locomotive speed, the numerous landscapes stretching about on every side, changing
as rapidly and charmingly as the views in the
kaleidoscope, keep the tourist rapt in a continual
state of enthusiastic admiration. The cool bracing atmosphere; the novelty of whirling along
the road at so great an elevation without any apparent motive power; the valley lying so far
below; the various ranges of hills and mountains
with their trees and vegetation in an endless
variety of colors, are all calculated to make
the beholder think himself in some enchanting
fairy-land. You may travel thousands of miles
and it will be difficult to find any other locality
so truly picturesque.

3*

HISTORY

Mining and Transportation Companies.

THE LEHIGH COAL AND NAVIGATION COMPANY.

In the year 1793 a company was formed under the title of the " Lehigh Coal Mine Company," who purchased from Jacob Weiss the tract of land on which the large opening at Summit Hill is made, and afterwards "took up" under warrants from the Commonwealth, about ten thousand acres of land, embracing about five-sixths of the coal lands now owned by the Lehigh Coal and Navigation Company. The Coal Mine Company proceeded to open the mines, and made an appropriation of ten pounds

($48.40) to construct a road from the mines to the landings (nine miles!!) After many fruitless attempts to get coal to market over this nominal road, and by the Lehigh river, which, in seasons of low water, in its unimproved state, defied the floating of a canoe over its rocky bed, and after calling for contributions of money from the stockholders until calling was useless, the Lehigh Coal Mine Company became tired of the experiment, and suffered their property to lie idle for some years.

In the meantime they endeavored to get the navigation of the Lehigh improved, and several laws were passed by the Commonwealth without effecting this object. To encourage and bring into notice the use of their coal, the Company, in December, 1807, gave a lease upon one of the coal veins to Rowland and Butland for twenty-one years, with the privilege of digging iron ore and coal *gratis*, for the manufacture of iron. This business was abandoned, together with the lease, as, from some cause, they did not succeed in their work.

In December, 1813, the Company made a lease

for ten years of their lands, to Messrs. Miner, Cist and Robinson, with the right of cutting lumber on the lands, for building boats; the whole consideration for this lease was to be the annual introduction into market of *tent housand bushels* of coal, for the benefit of the lessees. Five ark loads of coal were despatched by these gentlemen from the landing at Mauch Chunk, two of which reached Philadelphia, the others having been wrecked in their passage. Four dollars a ton were paid to a contractor for the hauling of this coal from the mines to the landing, and the contractor lost money. The principal part of the coal which arrived at Philadelphia was purchased at twenty-one dollars per ton, by White and Hazard, who were then manufacturing wire at the Falls of Schuylkill. But even this price did not remunerate the owners for their losses and expenses in getting the coal to market, and they were consequently compelled to abandon the prosecution of the business, and of course, did not comply with the terms of the lease.

In December, 1817, Josiah White and Erskine Hazard, being desirous of supplying their works with anthracite coal, and finding they could not obtain it as cheaply from the Schuylkill region as they were led to believe it could be procured from the Lehigh, determined that Josiah White should visit the Lehigh mines and river, and obtain the necessary information on the subject. In this visit he was joined by George F. A. Hauto. Upon their return, and making a favorable report, it was ascertained that the lease on the mining property was forfeited by *non user*, and that the law, the last of six which had been passed for the improvement of the navigation of the river, had just expired by its own limitation. Under these circumstances the Lehigh Coal Mine Company became completely dispirited, and executed a lease to Messrs. White, Hauto and Hazard, for twenty years, of their whole property, on the conditions that after a given time for preparation, they should deliver for their own benefit at least forty thousand bushels of coal annually in Philadelphia and the districts, and should pay upon demand *one ear of corn* as an annual rent for the property.

Having obtained the lease these gentlemen

applied to the Legislature for an act to authorize them to improve the navigation of the Lehigh. Their project was considered chimerical, the improvement of the Lehigh particularly being deemed impracticable, from the failure of the various companies who had undertaken it under previous laws. The act of 20th of March, 1818, however, gave these gentlemen the opportunity of " ruining themselves," as many members of the Legislature predicted would be the result of their undertaking. The great first and second anthracite coal regions were then entirely unknown as such. Coal had been found on the Summit Hill, where the great opening of the Lehigh Company now is, and also at the Beaver Meadows. But there was then no knowledge that there were in each location, continuous strata of coal, for many miles in extent, in each direction from these two points. Indeed the old Coal Mine Company for some years offered a bonus of two hundred dollars to any one who should discover coal on their lands, nearer to the Lehigh than the Summit Mines, but without its being claimed.

On the 10th of August, 1818, the "Lehigh Navigation Company" was formed, the full amount of stock, fifty thousand dollars ($50,000), having been subscribed. The work of opening navigation was immediately commenced.

On the 21st of October of the same yeor "The Lehigh Coal Company" was formed, with a capital of fifty-five thousand dollars ($55,000), for the purpose of making a road from the river to the mines, and of bringing coal to market by the new navigation. The road which now for nine miles constitutes the grading of the railroad to the Summit Mines, was laid out in the fall of 1818, and finished in 1819. This is believed to have been the first road ever laid out by an instrument, on the principle of dividing the whole descent into the whole distance, as regularly as the ground would admit of, and to have no undulation. It was intended for a railroad, as soon as the business would warrant the expense of placing rails upon it. A pair of horses would bring down from four to six tons upon it, in two wagons.

The Navigation Company having great difficulty in carrying on the work, sometimes the water being too low, and at other times the ice and high water injuring the unprotected dams and carrying away some of the sluice gates, found it necessary that more money should be raised or the work must be abandoned.

A difficulty also arose among the managers themselves, which resulted in White and Hazard making an arrangement with Hauto for his interest in the concern, on the 7th of March, 1820. On the 21st of April, following, the Lehigh Coal Company and the Lehigh Navigation Company agreed to amalgamate their interests, and to unite themselves into one company, under the title of the "Lehigh Navigation and Coal Company," provided the additional sum of twenty thousand dollars was subscribed to the stock by a given date. Of this sum nearly three-fifths was subscribed by White and Hazard. With this aid the navigation was repaired, and *three hundred and sixty-five tons of coal sent to Philadelphia, as the first fruits of the concern.* This quantity of coal completely stocked the market, and was with difficulty disposed of in the year

1820. It will be recollected that no anthracite coal came to market from any other source than the Lehigh before the year 1825, as a regular business.

On the 1st of May, 1821, a new arrangement of the whole concern took place, by which all the interests became more closely amalgamated. The title of the company was changed to "The Lehigh Coal and Navigation Company."

The boats used on the descending navigation consisted of square boxes, or arks, from sixteen to eighteen feet wide, and twenty to twenty-five feet long. They were steered with long oars like a raft. Boats of this description were used on the Lehigh till the end of the year 1831, in which year forty thousand nine hundred and sixty-six tons were sent down, which required so many boats to be built, that, if they had all been joined in one length, they would have extended more than thirteen miles. The boats made but one trip, and were then broken up in the city, and the planks sold for lumber, the spikes, hinges and other iron work, being returned to Mauch Chunk by land, a distance of eighty miles. The hands employed in running these boats walked back for two or three years, when rough wagons were placed on the roads by some of the tavern keepers, to carry them at reduced fares. The business of the company was now becoming so large that the time had arrived for changing the navigation of the Lehigh into a slack water navigation. For the same reason it was found difficult to keep the turnpike to the mines in good order without coating it with stone, and it was determined that the best economy would be to convert it into a railroad. The railroad from Mauch Chunk to the Summit Mines was commenced in January, and completely in operation in May, 1827. It is nine miles in length, and has a descent all the way from the Summit Mines to the river. The whole transportation of coal upon it was done by gravity, the empty cars being returned to the mines by mules which *rode down* with the coal. The Lehigh slack water navigation was first opened for use at the close of June, 1829. When the improvement of the Lehigh was demonstrated to be perfectly practicable, and the extensive coal field owned by them was no longer considered to be of problematical value, the Legislature of 1818 was censured for having granted such valuable privileges, and all the "craziness" of the original enterprise was lost sight of.

At the present time this company owns about six thousand five hundred acres of valuable coal lands, which are estimated to contain after allowing for faults in mining and waste, the enormous quantity of six hundred millions of tons of coal.

THE LEHIGH VALLEY RAILROAD COMPANY.

The Lehigh Valley Railroad Company, of which Hon. Asa Packer is President, has its general offices in Philadelphia and Mauch Chunk; this is one of the best managed and most successful Railroads in the United States, and does an immense and profitable business.

This road has been in operation since September, 1855, and has a capital stock of eighteen million dollars, which it now proposes to increase to twenty-four million dollars, to enable them to complete their road through to New York City. It also has in it its possession thousands of acres of coal lands, situated in the Wyoming, Mahanoy and Lehigh regions. The main line extends from Easton to Waverly, a distance of two hundred and six miles; the Erie Railway Company contemplate laying a third rail on their road from Elmira to Buffalo, and when the West Jersey Railroad, the extension of the Lehigh Valley Road, which is now being constructed from Easton to New York, is completed, there will be direct communication from the seaboard to the great lakes without breaking bulk. This, with its hundred miles of branches extending into all the various coal basins, will make it one of the greatest enterprises of our State.

According to the last annual report for 1871, this road has an equipment consisting of one hundred and ninety-two locomotives; one thousand freight cars; sixteen thousand (four wheel) coal cars; and a passenger equipment of nearly seventy-five cars.

The coal tonnage for the last year shows that it has a carrying capacity at this time, of over five million tons. By this route passengers from Philadelphia and New York are carried through to Elmira without change of cars, and to Niagara Falls, Chicago and points in the west, with but one change (at Elmira).

LEHIGH AND SUSQUEHANNA RAILROAD.

This road formerly ran from White Haven to Wilkesbarre; after the great freshet of June 4th and 5th, 1862, which totally destroyed navigation between White Haven and Mauch Chunk, it was deemed more economical to build a railroad between these points, than to replace the navigation. In 1867, the road was extended to Easton, forming what is now known as the Lehigh and Susquehanna Division of the Central Railroad of New Jersey, having been leased by them in the year 1871, and being now operated by that company. The importance of this corporation may be inferred from the fact that in 1871, it had an available equipment of seventy-two locomotives; ten thousand five hundred and ninety-two five ton coal cars; besides an ample number of cars for passengers and freight.

This road was built under the superintendence of Hon. John Leisenring. Of this company E. W. Clark, Esq., of Philadelphia, is President. The rails from Mauch Chunk to Easton are made of the best Bessemer steel, and the masonry work on the culverts and bridges is of the most substantial kind. The main line extends from Easton to Union Junction, in Luzerne county, a distance of about one hundred and five miles. Passengers by this route are carried from Philadelphia and New York without change of cars into the Lehigh and Wyoming Valleys.